Pigs
in the
House

Pigs in the House

by Steven Kroll
pictures by Tim Kirk

Parents Magazine Press

New York

A Parents Magazine
Read Aloud Original

Text copyright © 1983 by Steven Kroll.
Illustrations copyright © 1983 by Tim Kirk.
All rights reserved.
Printed in the United States of America.
10 9 8 7 6 5

Library of Congress Cataloging in Publication Data

Kroll, Steven.
Pigs in the house.

Summary: When three cute pigs get into the farmhouse,
total chaos results.
[1. Pigs—Fiction. 2. Farm life—Fiction. 3. Stories
in rhyme] I. Kirk, Tim, ill. II. Title.
PZ8.3.K899Pi 1983   [E]   83-13310
ISBN 0-8193-1111-1

To Uncle Bert, Aunt Esther,
Uncle Joe, Aunt Maggie,
Velma, Ed, Betty
and J.O.—*T.K.*

For Karen,
who shares my world—*S.K.*

In their pigpen
Nice and wide
Three cute pigs lived
Side by side.

Farmer Mack came
In one day
Fed the pigs and
Spread some hay.

He was running
Very late
And forgot to
Lock the gate.

With a breeze it
Opened wide
So the pigs just
Ran outside.

Mack was busy
Planting seeds
Bess, his wife, was
Pulling weeds.

Rex, the dog, was
Outside, too
Getting all the
Cows to moo.

No one saw or
Seemed to care
Pigs went up the
Farmhouse stairs.

First the den, look
What they found
Pressed some buttons
Trains went round!

Next the TV
Lots of noise
And a carton
Full of toys.

In the bedroom
They don't rest
Pigs put bedsprings
To the test.

Oh, the kitchen
Bubbly shakes
And three gooey
Layer cakes.

Now the attic
Look at that
Glasses, jewelry
Tall top hat.

And two trunks with
Masks and plumes
Just the things for
Great costumes!

Meantime, Farmer
Mack and Bess
Came back in for
Lunch and rest.

Just imagine
Their surprise
When the kitchen
Met their eyes.

Their fine bed looked
Like a sack
Their whole house was
Out of whack.

Mack and Bess climbed
Up the stairs
Shouting like ten
Angry bears.

As their shouts turned
To a roar
Pigs stood trembling
At the door.

Out they raced and
What a sight
Mack and Bess jumped
Back in fright.

Three strange creatures
Rushed away
No one could have
Made them stay.

Quickly Farmer
Mack and Bess
Ran outside but
Could not guess

Who it was they
Had to blame
Everything seemed
Just the same.

In their pigpen
Nice and wide
Pigs were resting
Side by side.

Though it had been
Fun to roam
It was good to
Be back home.

About the Author

STEVEN KROLL woke up one morning and looked around his messy house. "What a pigpen!" he said. That started him wondering what it would be like if there really were pigs running around. And so began PIGS IN THE HOUSE.

Steven Kroll has written more than two dozen children's books including, for Parents, OTTO, DIRTY FEET, and THE GOAT PARADE. He lives in New York City in what is now a very neat apartment.

About the Artist

TIM KIRK says that when he was a boy he used to visit his Uncle Bert's farm in California. Uncle Bert had no pigs, but he kept chickens and sheep which he let Tim ride. (The sheep, not the chickens!)

Tim Kirk's fantasy illustrations have won him five "Hugo" awards. He works for Walt Disney Productions designing, among other things, shows and attractions for Disneyland and Walt Disney World. He has illustrated many children's books including THE GOAT PARADE.